Stories of Gnomes & Goblins

Christopher Rawson

Adapted by Lesley Sims

Illustrated by
Stephen Cartwright

Reading Consultant: Alison Kelly
University of Surrey Roehampton

Contents

Chapter 1

The lazy gnome

Harold was a happy farmer,
until the day a gnome arrived.

"This place looks good!" said
the gnome. "I think I'll stay."
Harold couldn't get rid of him.

At first, the gnome helped on the farm. But one day he went on strike and refused to do anything. That wasn't all.

"From now on, I want half of everything you grow," he shouted at Harold.

Harold didn't like that at all. So he agreed but decided he would trick the gnome.

OK, you can have half the next crop. Do you want the top or bottom half?

Umm, the bottom half.

That spring, Harold planted wheat in his fields. At harvest time, Harold took the top of the wheat and had sacks full of grain. The gnome got stalks.

"Next year, I'll take the top of the crop," said the gnome. So, Harold planted turnips.

At harvest time, Harold had piles of turnips. The gnome got the top of the plant: leaves.

The gnome was very angry. "Next year, grow wheat again," he shouted. "You can cut half the field and I'll cut half. Whoever finishes first can take all the wheat."

A race?

Yes! And I'm small and fast, so I'll win.

When the wheat was ready to cut, Harold went to the village blacksmith. He had a plan, but it needed lots of thin iron rods.

The night before the race,
Harold crept out to his field.
He stuck the thin iron rods
among the wheat, on the
gnome's half of the field.

Next day, Harold's scythe
swished through the wheat
easily. But the gnome's scythe
kept hitting the rods.

This wheat is
very tough!

Every time the gnome tried
to cut the wheat, his scythe hit
a rod. Soon it would not cut at
all. The gnome was so angry,
he shouted at Harold.

How dare
you trick me
again. I'm
leaving!

In a temper, he threw down
the scythe and stormed off.
Harold never saw him again.

Chapter 2

Goblin Hill

Jessy was skipping in the
sun when she heard a tiny,
tiny cry.

"Help me! Please, help me!"

13

When she looked down,
there was a fairy, stuck in a
spider's web.

Jessy could hardly believe her eyes. Gently, she lifted the fairy from the web.

"Thank you, thank you!" cried the fairy. "I was going to Goblin Hill for a party. Would you like to come?"

Jessy's gran had told her
stories about Goblin Hill.
Not once had Jessy imagined
goblins actually lived there.

But, now she looked closely,
she saw a door.

You saved
my life. Would you
like tea with the king
and queen?

"Imagine going into the
hill!" said Jessy, but she was
far too big...

...until the fairy tapped her on the toe.

The fairy opened the door and led Jessy inside.

They arrived in the middle of
a goblin parade.

"It's to celebrate the return of
Prince Kester," said the fairy.

Prince Kester was very excited to meet Jessy. He had never seen a girl up close before.

He asked the goblin choir
to sing a song just for Jessy.
The royal band tried to play
along, but they kept playing
wrong notes.

"And now, the Balancing Elves!" said the king. Jessy clapped loudly. But they were more like Falling Elves.

The Balancing Elves were followed by the Juggling Pixies. They were even funnier than the clowns.

21

Finally, everyone sat down
to a huge picnic in
the shade of a
lollipop
tree.

Let the
feast begin!

"I must go," said Jessy, at last. "My mother will wonder where I am."

"Don't worry," said the king. "Time stands still here."

Jessy ran down the tunnel and rolled out of the door.

Outside, the grass was a jungle. Jessy was still the size of a bee.

But, as she stood up, Jessy shot to her usual size. She looked back at the hill. The door was nowhere to be seen.

Jessy shook her head. What a fantastic adventure, but would her friends ever believe her?

Chapter 3

A magic bridge

Jack had been walking for weeks. Today, the end of his journey was in sight. "The city of Oxford!" he cried.

As the sun was setting, he reached a bridge on the edge of the city. He was too tired to walk another step.

Jack took some straw from his sack to make a bed. He lay down on the bridge. Soon, he was snoring gently.

But Jack had fallen asleep on a pixie bridge. In the middle of the night, the pixies arrived.

They flew down and pulled pieces of straw from his bed. One pulled too hard. He woke Jack up.

Jack watched the pixies fly
away on the straw. He wished
he could follow them.

All at once, he could!

After a long flight,
they landed on
a chimney.
One by one,
the pixies
flew inside.
Jack followed.

He landed in an enormous
cellar, filled with partying
pixies. One gave him a silver
cup full of a fruity drink.

A band played and they danced all night. But, as the sun rose, everyone vanished. Jack fell asleep...

...and woke up back on the bridge. He thought it had been a dream, until he saw the silver cup.

I can't believe I spent the night dancing with pixies!

Jack tried to sell the cup to buy some breakfast. But the shopkeeper was horrified.

"Thief! Police!" yelled the man. Jack turned and fled. He didn't get very far.

Those pixies planted that cup on me!

Jack was taken to a judge who told him off.

"You slept on the pixies' bridge?" cried the judge. "Why didn't you say? You're free to go. Just be careful where you sleep from now on."

Chapter 4

Willo the Wisp

Every day, on his way home
from school, James saw a
strange light. It shone far
away over the marshes.

When he asked his mother about it, she turned pale.

"That's the candle of Willo the Wisp," she said. "Keep away!"

If you follow his light, you'll lose your way in the marshes and never come back.

For a whole week, James tried not to think about the light. But one night he just couldn't sleep. He crept from his bedroom and headed out onto the marsh.

A frightened frog croaked at him as he went by.

"Go back or Willo the Wisp will get you!" it warned. James went on.

A worried owl hooted at him as he went by.

"Go back or Willo the Wisp will get you!" it warned. James went on.

"If he catches you," called the owl, "blow out his candle. That breaks the spell."

James followed the light, deeper and deeper into the dangerous marsh. The light was getting closer...

James grabbed the candle
and blew
it out in
one puff.

Aaaggghhh!

As the flame went out,
James found he could move.
He turned and ran for home.

He ran past the worried owl.
"Thank you! You saved my
life," he told the owl.

I broke
the spell!

He ran past the frightened frog. "I wish I'd listened to you," he said to the frog. "I'll never visit the marshes again."

Back home, he scrambled up the tree to his bedroom.

Safe under the covers, James breathed a sigh of relief. He put Willo the Wisp's candle by his bed.

After that, whenever he felt curious about something, he looked at the candle. One look and his curiosity went out like a light.

Try these other books in
Series One:

Witches: Three tales about witches: one who loses her broomstick, one who loses her temper, and one who loses her cool with a clever farmer.

The Dinosaurs Next Door: Mr. Puff's house is full of amazing things. Best of all are the dinosaur eggs – until they begin to hatch...

Wizards: One wizard looks after orphans, one sells cures, and one must stop a band of robbers from taking the last sack of gold in the castle.

The Monster Gang: The Monster Gang is together for their first meeting in the treehouse. But one of the monsters hides a secret.

Series editor: Lesley Sims
Designed by Katarina Dragoslavic

This edition first published in 2006 by Usborne Publishing Ltd.,
Usborne House, 83-85 Saffron Hill, London EC1N 8RT, England.
www.usborne.com
Copyright © 2006, 2003, 1980 Usborne Publishing Ltd.